FRIENDSHIP CLUB

Strawberry Shortcake

The Friendship Trip

By Megan E. Bryant
Illustrated by Laura Thomas

Grosset & Dunlap

Visit www.strawberryshortcake.com to join the
Friendship Club and redeem your Strawberry
Shortcake Berry Points for "berry" fun stuff!

GROSSET & DUNLAP
Published by the Penguin Group
Penguin Group (USA) Inc., 375 Hudson Street, New York, New York 10014, U.S.A.
Penguin Group (Canada), 90 Eglinton Avenue East, Suite 700,
Toronto, Ontario, Canada M4P 2Y3
(a division of Pearson Penguin Canada Inc.)
Penguin Books Ltd, 80 Strand, London WC2R 0RL, England
Penguin Ireland, 25 St Stephen's Green, Dublin 2, Ireland
(a division of Penguin Books Ltd)
Penguin Group (Australia), 250 Camberwell Road, Camberwell,
Victoria 3124, Australia
(a division of Pearson Australia Group Pty Ltd)
Penguin Books India Pvt Ltd, 11 Community Centre,
Panchsheel Park, New Delhi - 110 017, India
Penguin Group (NZ), 67 Apollo Drive, Mairangi Bay,
Auckland 1311, New Zealand
(a division of Pearson New Zealand Ltd)
Penguin Books (South Africa) (Pty) Ltd, 24 Sturdee Avenue, Rosebank,
Johannesburg 2196, South Africa
Penguin Books Ltd, Registered Offices:
80 Strand, London WC2R 0RL, England

Strawberry Shortcake™ © 2007 by Those Characters From Cleveland, Inc. Used
under license by Penguin Young Readers Group. All rights reserved. Published
by Grosset & Dunlap, a division of Penguin Young Readers Group, 345 Hudson
Street, New York, New York 10014. GROSSET & DUNLAP is a trademark of
Penguin Group (USA) Inc. Printed in the U.S.A.

Library of Congress Control Number: 2006100773

ISBN 978-0-448-44557-1   10 9 8 7 6 5 4 3 2 1

Chapter 1

"It's so *hot!*" moaned Huckleberry Pie. He flopped down in the tall grass on the bank of the River Fudge. "How can anybody have fun outside when it's this hot?"

Strawberry Shortcake took a sip of lemonade. "Well, it's better than not having any fun inside, isn't it?" she joked.

"Here, Huck, have a sandwich," offered Orange Blossom.

"I don't want a sandwich," Huck

replied. He sounded grumpy. "I want to *do* something! But it's too hot to play any games. It's so hot, the fish aren't even biting. I wish it could be summer without being so hot!"

Strawberry had to agree. Summer was usually one of her favorite seasons. She loved going berry picking, having picnics, and spending long, lazy summer afternoons with her friends. But her favorite activities weren't quite as fun since a heat wave had hit Strawberryland.

"You know what, Huck?" Strawberry said. "You're right. Things have been berry boring around here lately! And I know the solution—a vacation!"

"A vacation?" asked Huck.

"Yes!" replied Strawberry. "That's exactly what you need. We all do! Let's have a meeting of the Friendship Club this afternoon to plan one!"

"Oooh!" Orange squealed. "A Friendship Club vacation is practically guaranteed to be the best vacation ever!"

Strawberry grinned. "Then what are we waiting for?" she asked. "Let's find the rest of our friends!"

An hour later, Strawberry skipped down the Berry Trail toward the Friendship Clubhouse. Ever since Strawberry had started the club—along with her best friends Huck, Orange, Blueberry Muffin, Ginger Snap, and Angel Cake—it seemed as if exciting adventures were always happening! Being a part of the Friendship Club meant that Strawberry and her friends got to spend even more time together—and do lots of fun things.

Strawberry slipped into the Clubhouse. "It's so cool in here!" she called out as she walked into the main room.

"That's because everyone brought fans to the meeting!" replied Blueberry Muffin.

Strawberry giggled as she put her backpack on the floor. "I brought one, too!"

"Well, great minds think alike, you know," Angel Cake said, laughing.

"Now that we're all here, can we start planning the vacation?" Huck burst out. He was so excited that he couldn't sit still. "I want to go to Tangerine Bosque!"

"And visit Tangerina Torta?" asked Orange. "That sounds like the best vacation ever! Oh, I'd love to go hiking in the rain forest and eat the tropical fruits she grows!"

"Yeah! It would be a real adventure!" Huck added.

Angel Cake wrinkled her nose. "But it will be *really* hot there, too. Wouldn't you guys rather visit Crêpes Suzette in Pearis?" she asked. "We could eat éclairs at a café and check out all the new fall fashions!"

"Fall fashions? That doesn't sound like an exciting vacation," Huck said. "But I would like those éclairs!"

"Anyway, we just saw Crêpes Suzette when she visited us last month," Ginger said. "I want to see a friend we haven't seen in a long time—like Tea Blossom!"

"Those are great ideas," Strawberry spoke up. "But there's one big problem with all of them."

"What's that?" asked Huck.

"All those places are berry far away," Strawberry continued. "It takes a long time to plan a trip to a faraway place. It could be weeks before we actually leave! I was hoping we could leave soon."

"Me too, I guess," Huck replied.

The friends were silent for a moment. Then a twinkle appeared in Strawberry's brown eyes. "I have an idea," she said slowly. "What if we went camping . . . on Ice Cream Island?"

"You mean where the fillies live?" asked Blueberry.

Strawberry nodded. "It would be the perfect trip! It's close by, so we could probably go next weekend. The island gets nice cool breezes. There are lots of trails and places to explore. And we haven't seen our filly friends in a while. It would be great to see them!"

"Yeah!" Huck yelled excitedly. "I love camping! I can't wait to pitch a tent and eat outside and—"

"And ride the fillies all over the island!" interrupted Ginger.

"And braid their manes with pretty ribbons!" Angel exclaimed.

Soon all the kids were laughing and chatting about the trip—except for Orange. She cleared her throat. "I don't know," she said in a soft voice.

But no one heard her.

Orange tried again. "I said, 'I don't know,' " she repeated. But still, no one looked at her. "I said, 'I don't know'—I mean *no*!" she said even louder.

Silence fell over the room. Orange could feel her face growing hot. "We should, um, talk a little more," she stammered. "Maybe—maybe we haven't thought of the perfect place yet."

"Well, I think Ice Cream Island is perfect," Huck said. "What's wrong with it?"

"Yeah," added Blueberry. "Why don't you want to go camping?"

"I thought you liked spending time outside," Ginger said.

"I—I do," Orange replied. "But maybe we should think about a different trip."

"Let's have a vote," suggested

Strawberry. "All in favor of going to Ice Cream Island, say 'aye.' "

"Aye!" chorused Huck, Blueberry, Angel, Ginger, and Strawberry.

"All against going to Ice Cream Island, say 'nay,' " Strawberry continued.

Everyone turned to look at Orange.

"Nay," she said quietly, staring at the ground.

"Aw, come on, Orange!" pleaded Huck. "Everybody else wants to go camping. Please?"

"I know you'll have a good time if you give it a chance!" Blueberry said encouragingly.

Orange looked at all the club members. How could she disappoint her friends? "Okay," she said, sighing. "Let's go camping."

"Hooray!" cheered everyone but Orange Blossom. They were so happy that they didn't notice the worried look in Orange's eyes.

"Let's start planning!" Strawberry said excitedly. She grabbed a notebook and a pen. "First we need someone to go to Ice Cream Island to tell the fillies about our trip. I can do that tomorrow."

"Sounds good, Strawberry," Ginger said.

"Someone should be in charge of organizing the trip," Strawberry continued.

"Me! Me!" volunteered Blueberry. "I can make checklists for everybody."

"Great!" Strawberry replied. "Who wants to be in charge of the food?"

"Oh, I do!" exclaimed Angel Cake.

"And who wants to get all the supplies?" asked Strawberry.

"I can!" replied Huck and Ginger at the same time. The kids laughed.

"That job is big enough for two people to share!" Strawberry said. She looked at her list. "I think that's it . . ."

"But Orange doesn't have a job," Angel spoke up.

"Oh, that's true!" Strawberry said. She turned to Orange. "What would you like to do to get ready for the trip?"

"Oh, I don't know," Orange said softly. "There probably isn't any—"

Suddenly Blueberry snapped her fingers. "I know! You can make a tent! That's practically the most important job—

because if we don't have a tent, where will we sleep?"

"A tent? I don't—" Orange began. But she was interrupted by Angel Cake's giggles.

"Strawberry! How could you forget the tent?" Angel asked.

Strawberry laughed, too. "It's a good thing we're all planning this trip together!" she said. "I'll put Orange down for the tent . . ."

"Wait. I don't even know how to make a tent!" Orange cried.

"But you're great at sewing," Angel said, a little bit confused.

"But—" protested Orange.

"I can help," offered Blueberry. "I'll find a pattern for us to follow and we can make a giant patchwork tent out of fabric scraps we already have."

Orange sank down in her seat. "All right," she replied with a sigh.

"Thanks, Orange," Strawberry said. She clapped her hands excitedly. "Everything is coming together so perfectly! I can't wait!"

Orange tried to smile at her friends. They all seemed so happy. She only wished that she could feel excited about the trip, too.

But going to Ice Cream Island was the last thing Orange wanted to do!

Chapter 2

After the meeting, Strawberry and Blueberry walked partway home together. Strawberry was still feeling giddy with excitement about the trip—but something was bothering her.

"Orange Blossom seemed kind of down today, didn't she?" Strawberry asked.

"Did she?" Blueberry replied. "Huh. I didn't really notice. She's always pretty quiet."

"I know—but this was different. It almost seemed like she didn't want to go on the trip." Strawberry bit her lip thoughtfully. "Maybe Orange will come with me to Ice Cream Island to let the fillies know about our plans. That might help her remember what a fun place it is!"

Blueberry nodded. "Yeah—it *has* been a while since we went there!" she said as the girls approached a fork in the Berry Trail. "Stay cool, Strawberry!"

"You, too!" Strawberry replied.

Strawberry called Orange Blossom as soon as she got home.

Brrring! Brrring! Brrring!

"Hello?" answered Orange.

"Hi! It's Strawberry!"

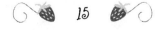

"Oh, hi!" said Orange. "I just got home from the meeting."

"Me, too," Strawberry replied. "Hey, would you like to come to Ice Cream Island with me tomorrow?"

"No!" Orange exclaimed. "I mean—"

"But it will be fun!" Strawberry said, trying to convince Orange. "We can see all the fillies and find a campsite."

"N-no, I just can't go," stammered Orange. "It's, um, too hot. I have to stay home to water my plants. They need lots of water when it's this hot. Actually, I need to go water them right now. I'll, uh, talk to you later, okay, Strawberry? Bye."

Click.

Strawberry stared at her pink cordless phone. Had Orange just hung up on her?

With a sigh, Strawberry put the phone on the counter.

Why didn't Orange want to go to Ice Cream Island?

Why didn't she want to spend time with her friends?

Early the next morning, Strawberry left for her trip to Ice Cream Island. When she set off on the Berry Trail the sky was still pink from the rising sun. Soon Strawberry reached the River Fudge. Just as planned, Huck had left his canoe for her to use. She paddled down the river until she reached the Soda Streams—pink, bubbling waters that cascaded down from the highest mountain and surrounded Ice Cream Island.

As Strawberry got closer to the island, she could see its rainbow-colored ice cream mountains glistening in the morning sun. Strawberry's heart pounded with excitement. She couldn't wait to see her filly friends—especially Honey Pie Pony! Strawberry paddled over to the edge of the water and dragged the canoe high onto the shore. She breathed in the crisp, cool air and raced to the Ice Cream Island stable.

As she ran into the clearing around the stable she called out, "Hello, Honey Pie Pony! Hello, everybody!"

Honey Pie looked up from the sweet clover she was nibbling. "Strawberry! Hello! What a nice surprise!" she said. "I didn't expect a visit from you today!"

The rest of the fillies whinnied happily. Strawberry could tell they were glad to see her, too, even if they weren't able to talk like Honey Pie Pony.

"It's good to see you, too!" Strawberry said as she threw her arms around Honey Pie's neck. "I have a lot to talk to you about!"

"Oooh, exciting!" Honey Pie exclaimed. "But do you want to go for a ride first?"

"Of course I do!" Strawberry replied. She hoisted herself onto Honey Pie's back and carefully held onto her golden mane as the filly began to trot out of the clearing. Honey Pie galloped along the trail, splashing through the Soda Streams on the way up the mountain.

"Oh! Honey Pie! I almost forgot!" Strawberry exclaimed suddenly when they

paused for a break. "I brought you a surprise."

"I had a feeling you did," Honey Pie replied slyly as Strawberry dismounted. "Is it my favorite . . . sugar cubes?"

Strawberry's eyes widened. "How did you know?" she asked as she pulled a brown paper bag out of her backpack. "Did you see them?"

"No—but I could smell them!" Honey Pie said as she nibbled the sugar cubes. "Delicious!"

"I wanted to ask you a question," Strawberry continued. "Would it be okay if the Friendship Club came to camp on Ice Cream Island this weekend?"

"Of course!" Honey Pie exclaimed. "It's been a long time since everybody visited us.

So, who's coming? You, Huck, Blueberry, Ginger, and Angel, I guess."

"And Orange Blossom," Strawberry reminded her.

Honey Pie looked surprised. "Really? Orange is coming, too?"

"Well, sure she is," said Strawberry. "Why wouldn't she?"

Honey Pie Pony looked away. "Oh, I don't know. No reason, I guess," she replied.

Strawberry frowned. Was Honey Pie keeping something from her? But before she could ask another question, Honey Pie changed the subject.

"We'd all love to have the Friendship Club come for a visit!" Honey Pie announced brightly. "And I know just where you should set up camp. Hop on and I'll take you there!"

Honey Pie galloped back toward the stables, with Strawberry holding on tight. "I think this clearing is the *perfect* place for camping," Honey Pie said. "The clover there will be soft and cushy under your sleeping bags, and nearby there's space for a campfire. And you'll have a beautiful view of the stars at night!"

"It looks great!" Strawberry said with a grin. "Oh, Honey Pie, I can't wait! I'd better get back to Strawberryland so I can start packing."

"Okay, Strawberry," Honey Pie replied. "See you soon—*very* soon!"

Chapter 3

Strawberryland was full of activity for the next few days. Blueberry Muffin had made checklists for each friend, and Strawberry put hers on the fridge right away so she wouldn't forget to do anything. She smiled every time she crossed a task off the list.

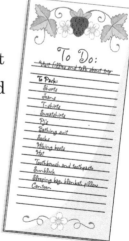

Straw-buh-buh-buh-berry! Strawberry's cell phone rang with her custom ring tone.

"Hello?" Strawberry answered the phone.

"Hey, it's Huck! Can you meet Ginger Snap and me at the Clubhouse?"

"Sure," replied Strawberry. "Is everything okay?"

"You bet!" Huck said. "See you in a few minutes!"

When Strawberry arrived at the Clubhouse, Huck and Ginger were waiting outside with grins on their faces.

"What's up?" Strawberry asked. "You guys look happy."

"Check out what we've done!" Ginger said. She grabbed Strawberry's arm and pulled her into the Clubhouse. It was filled with camping supplies!

"Wow!" Strawberry exclaimed. "Look at all this stuff! You've been really busy!"

ake sure we're not forgetting anything. Do

u mind calling Angel to tell her?"

"Sure, I'll call her," Blueberry said. "See

then, Strawberry."

Okay! Bye!" Strawberry replied.

ick.

awberry dialed Orange's phone

right away.

ing! Brrring! Brrring! Brrring!

answered.

erry hung up. She had a feeling

hing just wasn't right with

ssom.

was determined to find out

ge Blossom Acres, Orange

"We're keeping all the supplies here," Huck said. "So far we have a first-aid kit, a map, a compass, special supplies for cooking over a campfire, extra bags, flashlights and batteries, some tools, and a tarp to put under the tent!"

"Since Angel's bringing the food, and everyone else is bringing their own clothes and sleeping bags, all we need is the tent!" Ginger said. "But I think Orange is still working on it. I called her to see if it was ready yet, but she didn't answer."

"Well, this is all berry cool!" replied Strawberry. "I want to go on the trip even more now that I've seen all these supplies. Let's have the whole Friendship Club meet at the Clubhouse the night before we leave.

That way, we can make sure everybody has everything they'll need."

"Yeah!" Ginger agreed. "It will be fun to hang out the night before the trip, too."

"I'll call everyone to let them know," Strawberry said. "Great job, guys! See you on Friday night!"

When she got home, Strawberry called Blueberry first.

Brrring! Brrring! Brrring!

"Hello?" answered Blueberry.

"Hi! It's me, Strawberry!"

"Hi! What's up?" asked Blueberry.

"I was just at the Clubhouse with Huck and Ginger, and they've gotten together nearly everything they need for our camping trip!" Strawberry exclaimed.

"Wow! They worked fast!" B[lueberry] said. "We don't leave for two m[ore days?] Hey, have you talked to Oran[ge]

"No, I haven't," Strawbe[rry]

"Neither have I!" Blue[berry was?] going to help her make [?] I found a cool pattern [?] a bunch of different [?] every time I call he[r]

Strawberry fro[wned?] wonder if she st[ill?] is working so [?] going to help

"Maybe [?] sound co[?]

"Oh, [?] contin[ued?] ever[y?] Cl[ubhouse?]

didn't even hear the phone ring. That's because she was outside in the blazing sun, hoeing and raking a new patch for her garden. She wiped her forehead as she paused to take a quick break.

Orange never worked in her garden during the hottest part of the afternoon. But today,

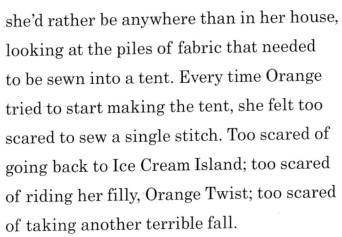

she'd rather be anywhere than in her house, looking at the piles of fabric that needed to be sewn into a tent. Every time Orange tried to start making the tent, she felt too scared to sew a single stitch. Too scared of going back to Ice Cream Island; too scared of riding her filly, Orange Twist; too scared of taking another terrible fall.

None of her friends knew that just a few weeks ago, Orange had visited Ice Cream

Island by herself.
Orange Twist was one
of the shyest, most
nervous fillies. She
was easily frightened
by loud noises or

surprises. Orange Blossom understood
her—because sometimes she felt shy and
nervous, too. That was one reason why they
were such good friends.

But on Orange Blossom's last visit to
the island, something awful had happened.
She had been riding Orange Twist when a
bird flew too close to Orange Twist's head.
Orange Twist was so frightened, she had
bucked—and thrown Orange Blossom right
off her back!

Luckily, Orange had landed in a soft
pile of hay. She had only a few bumps and

bruises from her fall. But she knew she would never forget how scary it had been to fly through the air.

Once Orange had realized she was okay, she had been furious at Orange Twist. In front of all the fillies, she had told Orange Twist that she never wanted to see her again. She went right home to her tree house in Orange Blossom Acres, and never told her friends about the big fall—or what she had said.

That day on Ice Cream Island had been one of the worst days of Orange Blossom's life. She just couldn't bear to go back there.

And that was why she hadn't even started making the tent—even though the trip was just two days away.

Chapter 4

On Friday night, Strawberry finished packing all the clothes she would need on the camping trip. Her sleeping bag was rolled and tied. She was ready to meet her friends at the Clubhouse—and she couldn't wait!

Strawberry put on her backpack, grabbed her duffel bag and sleeping bag, and set off for the Clubhouse. She walked there faster than usual.

"Hello? Anybody here?" Strawberry called out when she arrived. But there was no answer. Strawberry laughed to herself. "I guess I *am* a little early."

"I'm early, too!" said a voice behind Strawberry. It was Ginger Snap. "I ran all the way here," she said, trying to catch her breath. "I don't think I'm going to get any sleep tonight. I'm too excited!"

"I know! Me, too!" Strawberry exclaimed. "I wonder when everybody else will get here."

"Soon, I hope!" replied Ginger. "Maybe we can organize the camping supplies while we wait for them."

"Sure," Strawberry said. "Just tell me what to do."

For the next few minutes, Strawberry and Ginger carefully arranged the supplies into neat piles. Then they heard giggling on the path outside.

"Somebody's here!" Ginger said, her dark eyes shining. The girls ran over to the door.

Outside, Angel and Blueberry were carrying bags full of groceries, while Huck dragged a cooler behind him. "Ugh—Angel—this cooler is *heavy*! Maybe you made too much food," Huck teased her.

"You won't say that when it's time to eat!" Angel joked.

"Here, Huck, let me help," Ginger said as she grabbed the other end of the cooler. "Yikes! Angel, what are you planning to cook? Rocks?"

"Ha-ha, guys," Angel said. "Actually, the cooler is full of everything we need to make hot dogs, hamburgers, campfire stew, sausage and eggs for breakfast, and also—"

"Wow," said Huck. "I won't complain about the cooler being heavy anymore!"

"Look at all these supplies!" exclaimed Blueberry as she glanced around the room. "We have everything we need for the trip!"

"Except the tent," Ginger spoke up. "Where's Orange Blossom?"

"We're still waiting for her," Strawberry replied. "I left her a message about meeting up tonight—I'm sure she'll be here soon."

The kids chatted excitedly about the camping trip as they waited for Orange. But as the minutes ticked by, Orange did not arrive.

"Maybe Orange didn't get my message," Strawberry finally said.

"I can go to her house and bring her back," volunteered Ginger.

"Me, too!" added Blueberry.

"Thanks!" Strawberry replied. "We'll stay here and put away the food."

Strawberry, Angel, and Huck unloaded the items into the Clubhouse's fridge. Then they filled all the ice trays with water and put them in the freezer so that there would be enough ice for the cooler. By the time they finished, Blueberry and Ginger still weren't back.

"This is getting berry strange," Strawberry said. "Orange hasn't seemed like herself all week. But I can't figure out what's going on!"

Suddenly, the door burst open. It was Blueberry and Ginger—but Orange wasn't with them!

"We have to cancel the trip!" exclaimed Blueberry with tears in her eyes.

"What?" cried the other kids. Everyone began talking at once.

"Wait a minute!" Strawberry yelled, raising her hands. "Blueberry, what are you talking about? What's going on? And where's Orange Blossom?"

"Oh, she's at home," Ginger Snap said angrily. "She couldn't face everyone after what she did."

"What did she do?" Angel asked, her eyes wide.

"She never even bothered making the tent!" Ginger announced. "Everybody worked so hard all week, and Orange did *nothing*, and now we have no tent! How can we go camping without a tent?"

"I can't believe it!" exclaimed Strawberry. "That's not like Orange at all. What's gotten into her?"

"Who cares?" snapped Angel Cake. "She never wanted to go on this trip, and now she's ruined it for the rest of us."

"Yeah!" added Ginger. "It's probably better that the trip is canceled, because Orange would have had a bad attitude the whole time!"

"You don't know that," protested Strawberry. "And I'm sure we can find a way to go camping without a tent."

"But how?" Blueberry asked sadly.

"I promise I'll think of something," Strawberry said. "And I'm going to talk to Orange and find out what happened."

"You really think we can still go camping tomorrow, Strawberry?" Huck asked hopefully.

"I really do," she replied. "And I hope that Orange will be coming with us, too. It sounds like she's been having a tough time lately. So it's important for us to be berry good friends to her now. Okay?"

"Okay," Huck and Blueberry said. Angel and Ginger exchanged a glance before they finally agreed, too.

"Now, everybody go home and get some sleep," Strawberry said brightly. "We'll be leaving bright and early tomorrow morning!"

By the time everyone left the Friendship

Clubhouse, the kids were excited about the trip once more—except for Strawberry. In her heart, she was worried. How was she going to fix the tent problem *and* find out what was wrong with Orange Blossom in only one night?

"One thing at a time," Strawberry told herself. "I'll just go talk to Orange. Maybe, if I figure out what's bothering her, we can solve the tent problem together."

Twilight was falling as Strawberry climbed the twisty staircase up to Orange Blossom's tree house. She knocked on Orange's door. "Orange? It's Strawberry. Can I talk to you for a minute?"

There was a long pause. Strawberry began to think that Orange wasn't going to answer.

Then the door opened a crack as Orange

peeked out. "Strawberry, I'm really sorry that I didn't make the tent," she said. "But I don't want to talk to anybody, okay?"

"Orange, I don't care about the tent!" Strawberry said quickly before Orange could close the door. "I care about *you.* Is everything okay? You've seemed so sad lately. I want to help."

The door opened wider. "Well, come in, I guess," Orange said.

Strawberry followed Orange into the living room and sat next to her on the couch. The floor was covered with piles and piles of fabric pieces, in lots of colors and funky patterns. On the table, Orange's sewing machine was set up, along with dozens of spools of thread and shiny needles.

Orange looked around at all the sewing

supplies. "I tried," she said simply. "But I just couldn't do it."

"That's okay," Strawberry replied gently. "But why didn't you tell somebody? We're your friends. We would have understood. Maybe we could have helped."

"I *did* tell someone," Orange said, her voice shaky. "At the meeting—but no one was listening. Just like no one listened when I said I didn't want to go to Ice Cream Island."

"Orange, if you don't want to go on vacation with us, you don't have to. I just don't understand why you don't want to come," Strawberry said, putting an arm around her friend. "And nobody could imagine a Friendship Trip without you."

Orange stared at the floor, but she didn't say anything. After a long silence,

Strawberry sighed and stood up. "Okay, Orange," she said. "I'll call you when we get back. Bye."

As Orange watched Strawberry walk to the door, she knew she had only one more chance to go on the trip—and try to fix things with her friends. "Wait!" she cried. "I do want to go on vacation with everybody. It's just—I mean—"

"Really?" Strawberry exclaimed. "Oh, Orange, I'm so glad! We're going to have a great time, I promise!" She gave Orange a big hug. "Now we just have to figure out how we can camp without a tent."

"What if we slept in the extra stalls in the fillies' stable?" Orange asked. "Then we wouldn't have to worry about being outside without any covering."

"Orange, you're a genius!" Strawberry

announced. "There are lots of empty stalls in that big stable. We can turn them into forts by putting blankets over the top! It will be really cool! Now, do you still have your checklist? Do you need any help packing?"

"I don't think so," Orange said.

"Okay, then!" replied Strawberry. "I'll tell everyone to bring a blanket, and I'll see you early in the morning. Bye, Orange! We're going to have a great time!"

As she closed the door behind her friend, Orange hoped that Strawberry was right. She knew that her fear of riding Orange Twist was hurting her friendships. She knew that she had to find a way to not be so scared.

But she just couldn't figure out how.

Chapter 5

Early the next morning, all the kids met at the Friendship Clubhouse. Each was carrying an extra blanket—and looking sleepy.

"Why did we decide to leave so early?" Huck asked, rubbing his eyes.

"So that we'd have time for even more fun today!" Strawberry sang out. "You don't want to sleep through the camping trip, do you?"

"Some camping trip," Huck grumbled. "We won't even be sleeping in a real tent."

"I think building forts in the stable will be fun!" Blueberry Muffin said quickly when she saw how upset Orange looked. "It might be even better than sleeping in a tent!"

Huck just shrugged and started walking down the Berry Trail.

"Hey, Ginger," Orange said quietly. "Want to walk together?"

Ginger looked away. "Actually, um, I already told Angel I'd walk with her," she said. "Sorry."

Strawberry sighed as Orange Blossom fell to the back of the group by herself. It seemed that her friends weren't as ready to forgive Orange as Strawberry had hoped.

"Don't worry, Orange," Strawberry said

in a quiet voice. "Once we're on Ice Cream Island and having fun, everything will be back to normal!"

"I hope you're right," Orange whispered back. "Otherwise it's going to be a berry long trip!"

As the sun rose higher in the sky, Blueberry handed out delicious blueberry muffins that she had baked. The kids started laughing and telling stories. The trouble with Orange Blossom seemed to be forgotten. At last, the group crossed the Soda Streams and set foot on Ice Cream Island.

"Yeah! We're finally here!" Huck cheered, his grumpiness forgotten.

"I can't wait to see the fillies!" cried Blueberry.

"Come on! Come on!" squealed Angel

Cake as she started running to the stables. The rest of the kids followed her. Even Orange was excited to have finally arrived.

The fillies—Honey Pie Pony, Cookie Dough, Milkshake, Huckleberry Hash, Blueberry Sundae, and Orange Twist— were waiting for them in a clearing. From all the head-shaking, foot-stomping, and whinnying, it was clear that the fillies were just as excited as the kids!

"Hi there, Honey Pie!" called Strawberry.

"Strawberry! We're so glad you're *finally* here!" Honey Pie exclaimed.

"So are we," Strawberry replied, laughing.

All around the clearing, the kids greeted their special fillies. Huck had already climbed onto Huckleberry Hash's back. Angel was showing Milkshake a beautiful

new ribbon she'd brought for her. Ginger
Snap fed a sugar cube to Cookie Dough.
Blueberry Muffin gave Blueberry Sundae a
big hug.

But Orange held back shyly. She wasn't
ready to spend time with Orange Twist . . .
not yet, anyway. So she pretended to be
busy stacking all the camping supplies and
duffel bags.

"Who wants to go for a ride?" Huck
yelled as Hash bucked. "Yee-haw!"

"Strawberry, let's take everybody over the Soda Streams and up the mountain!" suggested Honey Pie.

"That's a great idea!" exclaimed Strawberry.

"Let me grab some picnic food," said Angel Cake.

Orange's heart sank. "Well—wait—can't we—shouldn't we set up camp first?" she stammered, her face burning.

"But we just got here!" Huck protested. "I want to do something fun."

"We'll have plenty of time to set up this afternoon, Orange," Blueberry said.

"But I really want to unpack before I do anything with the fillies," she continued, trying to find the right words.

The kids fell silent. Ginger Snap strode

over to Orange and whispered, "You're being rude, Orange! What's going on with you?"

Strawberry cleared her throat. "Um, Orange, everyone else wants to go for a ride and have a picnic. If you don't want to come, you can stay here and start setting up camp. Okay?"

"Okay," Orange mumbled, staring at the ground. She didn't watch the other kids mount their fillies. She didn't see Orange Twist sadly walk behind the stable. She didn't look up until the *clomp-clomp-clomp* of the fillies' hooves had faded into the distance.

And then she was all alone.

"It's all my own fault," she said angrily as she kicked a pebble. "I don't know how many second chances everybody is going to give me! I don't want to lose all my friends just because I'm scared of riding Orange Twist again!"

Suddenly, Orange realized that she could stand around feeling sorry for herself, or she could get the campsite ready for her friends. "They might be hungry and tired by the time they get back—and won't they be happy if everything is ready for them?" she said excitedly. And without wasting another moment, Orange got right to work. In the stables, she found six empty stalls. She swept them out, unrolled each sleeping bag in a separate stall, and put away her friends' duffel bags. Finally, Orange draped a blanket over the top of each stall. "Blueberry was right—this is a berry cool fort!" she said. "I hope everyone else thinks so, too."

Orange moved all the food into its own stall so it would be safe from woodland animals. She gathered some big, smooth rocks to build a fire pit. Then she found all the dry twigs and sticks she could so that the kids could have a campfire at night. By the time she was done, the campsite was ready—and it couldn't have been better! Orange was proud of all her hard work. And she was starting to feel hungry, too. As she rummaged in the cooler for some lunch, she tried not to think of the fun everyone else was having on the picnic.

When Orange went back outside with a sandwich and an apple, there was a strong breeze blowing. She looked up to see dark storm clouds heading straight for Ice Cream Island. "Wow—it looks like we're finally going to get that summer rain we've been missing," Orange said.

Then she had a terrible thought. If the storm turned into a downpour, the Soda Streams might flood—and her friends would be stranded at the top of the mountain!

Orange knew her friends would be having too much fun to notice the storm clouds. She had to warn them about the storm and bring them back to camp. But how? Her friends were riding on horseback. Even if she ran as fast as she could, Orange wouldn't catch up to them. "What am I going to do?" Orange cried. "I'll never reach them in time!"

Suddenly, a soft whicker from the bushes caught her attention. Shyly, Orange Twist stepped into the clearing.

Then Orange Blossom knew exactly what she had to do. If Orange Twist rode her up the mountain, she'd surely reach her friends before the storm.

Orange was still afraid. But the thought of her friends in trouble helped Orange push the fear to the back of her mind. "Hey, girl," she said softly as she whistled to Orange Twist. "Can you take me up the mountain?"

Orange Twist hesitated. She was worried that Orange Blossom was still mad at her.

"I'm so sorry I yelled at you, girl. I was just so scared! Can you forgive me?" Orange Blossom asked. She knew her filly friend hadn't meant to scare her.

Orange Twist forgave her immediately. She nickered and leaned down so Orange Blossom could climb on her back.

Orange took a deep breath. She placed her hands on Orange Twist's back and hoisted herself up. "We can do this, right, girl?" Orange Blossom said as she ran her fingers through Orange Twist's silky mane. "Let's just go easy . . . *giddyap*!"

Orange Twist pranced out of the clearing and then started to pick up speed. Orange Blossom held on tight and squeezed her eyes shut. She couldn't bear to look! But as Orange Twist galloped along the trail, Orange Blossom started to relax. All

the happy memories of riding Orange Twist came rushing back to her— until she had nearly forgotten about her big fall.

"You're doing great, girl!" Orange shouted into the wind. It didn't take long for them to reach the top of the mountain, where the kids and the fillies were about to have their picnic.

"Orange!" exclaimed Strawberry. "Did you change your mind?"

"Whoa, Orange Twist, whoa," Orange said as her filly stamped at the ground. "There's a big storm coming in from the south—look at those clouds heading toward us! If it rains too much, the Soda Streams could flood—and you wouldn't be able to come back down the mountain."

"Uh-oh—we need to leave right away!" Blueberry said. "Let's go!"

"Thank goodness you came, Orange! We

never would have seen those clouds in time," Strawberry cried as she hugged her friend.

The kids packed up their picnic and mounted their fillies. They began to ride down the mountain just as the first raindrops started to fall. By the time they reached the Soda Streams, the water had already started to rise. But it was still low enough that the fillies could charge through it.

"All right!" Huck yelled as water splashed over them. "This is awesome!"

By the time the kids returned to the stables, they were dripping wet. The clearing was covered in mud puddles.

"Th-this is awful!" Angel Cake said, her teeth chattering. "I'm s-so wet!"

"Hurry and come inside!" Orange yelled from the stable doorway.

"Orange!" Strawberry exclaimed when she

walked into the stable. "You did such a great job setting up camp!"

"If you hadn't brought our stuff inside, it would have gotten soaked!" Blueberry realized.

"You definitely saved the day," Huck added.

Orange Blossom smiled. "Let's get some dry clothes and get our fillies settled," she said. "Then we can have our picnic—inside!"

The kids changed quickly, then brushed their fillies and covered them with cozy blankets. They sat in a circle on the floor and passed around sandwiches, apples, carrots, and cookies.

Before Orange started eating, she looked around the circle at her friends. "Hey, everybody," she said. "I'm really sorry about how weird I acted last week. I'm sorry I didn't make the tent after I said I would. You were right—I didn't really want to come on the trip. But not because I didn't want to spend time with my friends!"

"Then why?" asked Blueberry quietly.

"I was—I was scared," Orange replied. "I never told anybody this, but a few weeks ago I came to visit Orange Twist. She got spooked while we were riding, and I fell. It was awful! And it made me never want to ride Orange Twist again."

"Oh, Orange, that sounds so scary!" Strawberry exclaimed. "No wonder you didn't want to come here."

"Yeah!" agreed Angel Cake as she put her arm around Orange. "But why didn't you tell us? We would have understood."

"I was really embarrassed!" Orange said with a shrug. "I didn't want to talk about it with anybody."

"And we didn't do a very good job of listening when you told us you didn't want to come to Ice Cream Island," Strawberry said. "I'm sorry, Orange. But you know what? Even though you were scared, you picked yourself up and tried again to help your friends. That's berry cool!"

"Yeah!" chorused the rest of the kids.

"And sleeping in the stables is going to be even better than sleeping in a tent since it's so wet outside," Huck added.

Orange grinned. "Hey! Did you hear that?" she asked suddenly.

"No—what?" Blueberry replied.

"I think the rain's stopped!" Orange ran over to the stable doors just in time to see the sun peeking through the last of the dark clouds. "We can look for constellations tonight!"

"And tomorrow we can go swimming!"

"And hiking!"

"And ride the fillies!"

Strawberry smiled as her friends—*all* of her friends—started talking excitedly about their plans for the next day. At the beginning, the trip had been a little rocky—but with her berry best friends around, it had turned out even better than she could have imagined!